ANDY
AND THE
LION

A TALE OF
KINDNESS REMEMBERED
OR
THE POWER OF GRATITUDE

BY

JAMES
DAUGHERTY

VIKING KESTREL

TO LADY ASTOR AND LORD LENOX, THE LIBRARY LIONS
WHO HAVE SO LONG SAT IN FRONT OF THE NEW YORK PUBLIC LIBRARY
AND WITH SUCH COMPLACENT GOOD NATURE AND FORBEARANCE
LOOKED DOWN ON MANHATTAN PARADE

VIKING KESTREL
Viking Penguin Inc., 40 West 23rd Street, New York, New York 10010, U.S.A.
Penguin Books Ltd, 27 Wrights Lane, London W8 5TZ (Publishing & Editorial) and
Harmondsworth, Middlesex, England (Distribution & Warehouse)
Penguin Books Australia Ltd, Ringwood, Victoria, Australia
Penguin Books Canada Limited, 2801 John Street, Markham, Ontario,
Canada L3R 1B4
Penguin Books (N.Z.) Ltd, 182-190 Wairau Road, Auckland 10, New Zealand

IT WAS A BRIGHT DAY WITH JUST ENOUGH

WIND TO FLOAT A FLAG. ANDY STARTED DOWN

TO THE LIBRARY TO GET

A BOOK ABOUT LIONS. HE TOOK THE BOOK

HOME AND

READ AND READ. ANDY READ ALL THROUGH

SUPPER AND

HE READ ALL EVENING AND JUST BEFORE BED

TIME

HIS GRANDFATHER TOLD HIM SOME TALL

STORIES ABOUT HUNTING LIONS IN AFRICA.

EVERY STORY ENDED WITH "AND THEN I GAVE

HIM BOTH BAR-R-R-E-L-L-S!" THAT NIGHT

ANDY DREAMED ALL NIGHT LONG THAT HE WAS

IN AFRICA HUNTING LIONS. WHEN AT LAST

MORNING CAME

ANDY WOKE UP. THE SUN WAS LOOKING IN AT
THE WINDOW AND PRINCE WAS TUGGING AT
THE BED CLOTHES. THE LIONS HAD LEFT BUT
ANDY KEPT THINKING ABOUT THEM.

ANDY THOUGHT LIONS ON THE BACK PORCH

AND HIS FATHER HAD TO REMIND HIM TO

WASH BEHIND HIS EARS.

ANDY WAS STILL THINKING LIONS AFTER

BREAKFAST WHEN HIS MOTHER GAVE HIS HAIR

A FINAL BRUSH AND

ANDY STARTED OFF TO SCHOOL.

PART

2

ANDY WALKED ALONG SWINGING HIS BOOKS

AND WHISTLING A TUNE. AS HE CAME TO THE

TURN IN THE ROAD HE NOTICED SOMETHING

STICKING OUT FROM BEHIND THE BIG ROCK

JUST AT THE BEND. IT LOOKED VERY QUEER SO

ANDY AND PRINCE CREPT UP CAUTIOUSLY TO

INVESTIGATE.

IT MOVED!

IT WAS A LION! AT THIS MOMENT

ANDY THOUGHT HE'D BETTER BE GOING AND

THE LION THOUGHT SO TOO. THEY RAN AND

RAN AROUND THE ROCK.

WHICHEVER WAY THAT ANDY RAN—THERE WAS

THE LION. WHICHEVER WAY THE LION RAN—

THERE WAS ANDY.

AT LAST THEY BOTH STOPPED FOR BREATH. THE

LION HELD OUT HIS PAW TO SHOW ANDY WHAT

WAS THE MATTER. IT WAS A BIG THORN STUCK

IN HIS PAW. BUT

ANDY HAD AN IDEA. HE TOLD THE LION TO

JUST BE PATIENT AND THEY'D HAVE THAT

THORN OUT IN NO TIME. FORTUNATELY

ANDY ALWAYS CARRIED HIS PLIERS IN THE BACK

POCKET OF HIS OVERALLS. HE TOOK THEM OUT

AND GOT A TIGHT GRIP. THEN

ANDY BRACED ONE FOOT AGAINST THE LION'S

PAW AND PULLED WITH ALL HIS MIGHT UNTIL

THE THORN

CAME

OUT.

THE GRATEFUL LION LICKED ANDY'S FACE TO

SHOW HOW PLEASED HE WAS.

BUT IT WAS TIME TO PART. SO THEY WAVED
GOOD—BY. ANDY WENT ON TO SCHOOL AND
THE LION WENT OFF ABOUT THE BUSINESS OF
BEING A LION.

IN THE SPRING THE CIRCUS CAME TO TOWN.

OF COURSE ANDY WENT. HE WANTED TO SEE

THE FAMOUS LION ACT. RIGHT IN THE MIDDLE

OF THE ACT THE BIGGEST LION

JUMPED OUT OF THE HIGH STEEL CAGE AND
WITH A TERRIBLE ROAR DASHED STRAIGHT
TOWARD THE PEOPLE. THEY RAN FOR THEIR
LIVES AND IN THE SCRAMBLE ANDY FOUND
HIMSELF

RIGHT IN THE LION'S PATH. HE THOUGHT HIS

LAST MOMENT HAD COME. BUT THEN

WHO SHOULD IT BE BUT ANDY'S OWN LION.

THEY RECOGNIZED EACH OTHER

AND DANCED FOR JOY. WHEN THE CROWD

CAME BACK READY TO FIGHT THE LION AND

CAPTURE HIM

ANDY STOOD IN FRONT OF THE LION AND

SHOUTED TO THE ANGRY PEOPLE:

"DO NOT HURT THIS LION. HE'S A FRIEND OF

MINE."

THEN THE NEXT DAY ANDY LED THE LION AND ALL THE

PEOPLE IN A GRAND PARADE DOWN MAIN STREET TO

THE CITY HALL. THERE THE MAYOR PRESENTED

ANDY WITH A MEDAL FOR BRAVERY. AND THE

LION WAS VERY MUCH PLEASED. AND THE

NEXT DAY

ANDY TOOK THE BOOK BACK TO THE LIBRARY.